THE NEW GIRL

WRITTEN BY MICHÈLE DUFRESNE · ILLUSTRATED BY ANN CARANCI

CONTENTS

PIONEER VALLEY EDUCATIONAL PRESS, INC.

CHAPTER ONE — NICOLE

One day, the principal
came into Jordan's classroom.

"Boys and girls," said the principal,
"this is Nicole. She has just
   moved here. She is
   going to be in your class."

"Hello, Nicole," said Jordan's teacher.
"Welcome to Room 3.
   You can sit next to Jordan.
   Jordan, please be Nicole's buddy
   and show her how
   we do things in Room 3."

Jordan waved to Nicole.
Nicole walked to Jordan's table
and sat down.

"Hi," said Jordan with a smile.

"Hi," said Nicole. But she did
not smile back at Jordan.
She looked sad.

"We are doing math,"
said Jordan.

"OK," said Nicole.
She took out a pencil
and began to work.

Jordan looked at Nicole as she
worked on the math problems.
She wished she had long black hair
like Nicole's. It was so pretty.
"I like your hair," said Jordan.

"Thanks," said Nicole.
"I get it cut at Georgio's,
  in the city."

"Oh," said Jordan.
She didn't know about Georgio's
in the city. Her mother cut her hair.

At lunch time, Jordan
showed Nicole the lunchroom.

Jordan took a peanut butter
and jelly sandwich out of her
lunch box. Next, she took out
some chocolate chip cookies
her mother had made.

Nicole took out her salad
and poured some dressing on it.
Then she looked at Jordan's
lunch. "My mother says salads
are much better for you.
Peanut butter and cookies
have a lot of calories in them."

At recess, Nicole told all the girls about her old school.

"It was in the city," she said.

"We wore uniforms, and I walked home every day for lunch.

On the weekend, we went shopping or to the art museum."

"Wow!" said one of the girls.
"That sounds like fun."

"That is so cool!
What did your uniforms look like?"
asked another girl.

CHAPTER TWO COWS AND CHICKENS

That night at dinner, Jordan told her family about the new girl.

"Why don't you ask her to come over after school to play?" asked Jordan's mom.

"Oh, no," said Jordan.

"Why not?" asked her dad.

"Well, she used to live in the city.
 We just live on a farm with chickens
 and cows," said Jordan.
"There is nothing fun to do here."

"There isn't?" asked her father.

"Chickens and cows are cool,"
  said Jordan's brother.
"Just as cool as anything in a city."

"I don't think so," said Jordan.
"She gets her hair cut in the city
  at Georgio's."

  Jordan's mother laughed.
"Do you think that is better
  than my haircuts?"

"Well," said Jordan.
"Her hair is very pretty."

"So is your hair," said Jordan's father.

The next day, Nicole
sat down next to Jordan.

"Hi," said Jordan.

"Hi," said Nicole.
Nicole did not smile.
She still looked very sad.

Jordan thought about asking Nicole
to come over after school to play.
But then she thought about
the cows and chickens,
and Georgio's in the city.

The teacher said, "It is time for silent reading. Please take out a book and start reading."

"Oh," said Nicole. "I need a book."

"I have two books if you want to read one of mine," said Jordan. "But you might not like them." She pulled two books about horses out of her backpack.

Nicole smiled for the first time.
"I love books about horses.
I've always wanted
to ride a horse."

"You have?" said Jordan.
"You like horses?"
The two girls began to talk
about their favorite horse books.

"Shhh," said the teacher.
"It's silent reading time!"

"Do you want to come over to play
at my house one day after school?"
whispered Jordan.

"Yes," whispered Nicole back.
"Will there be any of those delicious-
  looking cookies you had for lunch?"

"Sure," said Jordan.

"What will we do?" asked Nicole.

"We will think of something fun,"
  said Jordan with a big smile.

The next day, Nicole got off the bus with Jordan. "Is that your pony? Cool!" exclaimed Nicole.

"Yes," smiled Jordan.
"This is my pony, Marshmallow.
Do you want to ride him?"

"Wow, yes!" said Nicole.
"Ponies rock! You are so lucky!
What a great place this is!"